The author would like to thank Dr Gerald Legg
of the Booth Museum of Natural History, Brighton, for his help and advice

For Faye and Paul – J. B.

VIKING

Published by the Penguin Group
Penguin Books Ltd, 27 Wrights Lane, London W8 5TZ, England
Penguin Books USA Inc., 375 Hudson Street, New York, New York 10014, USA
Penguin Books Australia Ltd, Ringwood, Victoria, Australia
Penguin Books Canada Ltd, 10 Alcorn Avenue, Toronto, Ontario, Canada M4V 3B2
Penguin Books (NZ) Ltd, 182–190 Wairau Road, Auckland 10, New Zealand

Penguin Books Ltd, Registered Offices: Harmondsworth, Middlesex, England

First published 1994
1 3 5 7 9 10 8 6 4 2
First edition

Filmset in Weiss

A CIP catalogue record for this book is available from the British Library

ISBN 0-670-85052-7

PRINTED IN BELGIUM BY
proost
INTERNATIONAL BOOK PRODUCTION

THERESA RADCLIFFE

The SNOW LEOPARD

Illustrated by

JOHN BUTLER

VIKING

It was dawn. A pale sun rose between the mountains, turning the sky to silver. Samu the snow leopard lay stretched out on a frozen boulder, waiting to see what the light would bring. Little Ka sat watching at his mother's side.

A dark shape soared across the cliff face, gliding down on huge wings. Then came another, and another. Vultures were moving in, circling closer and closer to where the dead sheep lay. Samu leapt from the boulder and bounded down the slope towards the great birds. Ka darted back to a safe place in the rocks.

Samu reached the sheep and stood over it, lashing her tail until the last of the birds had gone. She had been guarding her kill for three days now. Only a little meat remained, but every last bit was precious. It was becoming harder and harder to find enough food for herself and her cub.

After a while, Ka crept out from the rocks and joined her.
He tumbled down the slope, scattering the loose stones.
He rubbed himself against her, then lay down and began to eat.

Samu took Ka to the top of a high crag. A single line of sheep were already moving down the far slopes. But Samu saw something else moving — slowly at first, then breaking into a run — wolves!

Wolves had come to the valley.

Samu knew that she and Ka could not follow the sheep now. They would have to find new herds in more distant pastures. It would be a difficult, dangerous journey with a young cub.

As the day wore on, an icy wind tore across the slopes. The first flakes of snow began to fall, thicker and thicker, covering the stony ground. The snows had come early.

Samu knew the sheep would be leaving the mountain to find grass in the lower pastures. She and Ka must follow them, if they were not to starve.

As night fell, the wind howled around the crag, bringing more snow. Samu and Ka crept between the rocks. While Ka slept, Samu stared out into the shining darkness, wondering when she would find food again.

Samu led her cub on. It was already dusk when they reached the High Pass. They would find no shelter now, until they had crossed this frozen waste of rock and ice. As they set out, the blizzard returned. Samu shielded Ka as best she could, but the icy winds and blinding snow whirled around them, tearing at their fur and stinging their eyes.

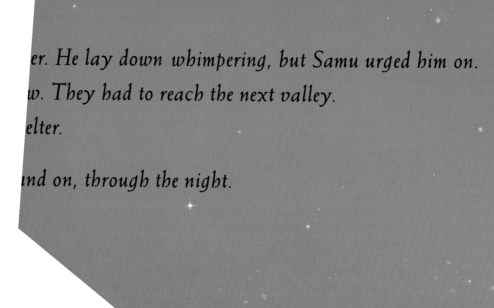

...er. He lay down whimpering, but Samu urged him on.

...w. They had to reach the next valley.

...elter.

...nd on, through the night.

At last they came to an outcrop of rocks. It was morning and the blizzard was over. They were safe now, Ka could rest. A herd of sheep grazed peacefully in the valley below. Here was food for the tired, hungry cub. Leaving Ka in the shelter of the rocks, Samu began to creep slowly and silently down the mountain towards the herd.